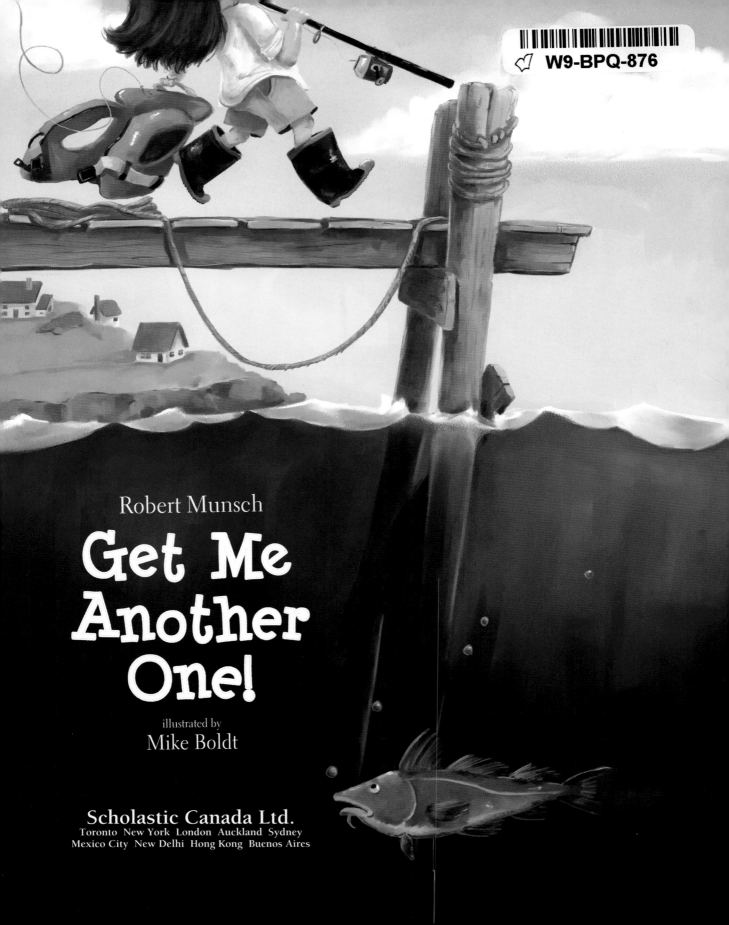

Robert Munsch

Get Me Another One!

illustrated by
Mike Boldt

Scholastic Canada Ltd.
Toronto New York London Auckland Sydney
Mexico City New Delhi Hong Kong Buenos Aires

Kristi sat at the end of the dock and yelled to her father, "Daddy, I want to go fishing in a boat. Everybody else in Rocky Harbour goes fishing in a boat."

2

Her father yelled back, "You are just a little kid. You are one of the littlest kids I know and you would probably fall into the ocean."

But Kristi said, "No, no, I will hang on. I will wear a life jacket. I will be very careful."

Her father thought for a while and said, "Ahhhhhh, okay."

Kristi was having a wonderful time out on the ocean, but then it started to get windy and the boat went up and down like this:
LAAA, LAAA, LAAA, LAAA, LAAA, LAAA

Kristi said, "I don't feel so good."
And her father said, "Uh-oh!"

Then it got windier and the waves got bigger and the boat went up and down like this:

LAAA, LAAA, LAAA, LAAA, LAAA, LAAA

Kristi said, "I feel sick."
"Yikes," said her father.
Then it got really windy and the waves got really big and the boat went up and down like this:

LAAAA, LAAAA, LAAAA, LAAAA, LAAAA, LAAAA

Kristi said, "Daddy, I think I'm going to throw up!"

"Oh no!" said her father. "Not in my clean boat! If you're going to throw up, throw up over the side."

So Kristi leaned over the side of the boat. A big wave came and she fell right into the ocean.

"OH NO!" yelled Kristi's father. He turned the boat around and went back to get Kristi.

He grabbed her by the collar and pulled as hard as he could, but he could not lift her out of the water.

He said, "Kristi, you're just a little kid. Why can't I get you into the boat?"

"Well," said Kristi, "I have a hold of the tail of an enormous fish."

"Good," said her father. "Keep a hold of that fish." He took the hook off his fishing line and tied the line to Kristi's ear. Then he pulled as hard as he could and Kristi came flying into the boat. She was holding a codfish that was two metres long.

"Look at this fish!" said Kristi. "It's fantastic!"

"It's incredible," said her father. "You're great at fishing!"

"Let's take it home and show it to Mommy," said Kristi.

"Wait!" said her father. "We've only caught one fish. We should get more."

"Sure!" said Kristi. "I love fishing!"

So her father said, "Then go get me another one," and he picked up Kristi and threw her back into the ocean.

Kristi swam around and around and then dove under the water.

She came up again and said, "I got a fish!
I got a fish! I got a fish!"

Kristi's father tied the line to her ear and
pulled as hard as he could, but he could
not get Kristi into the boat.

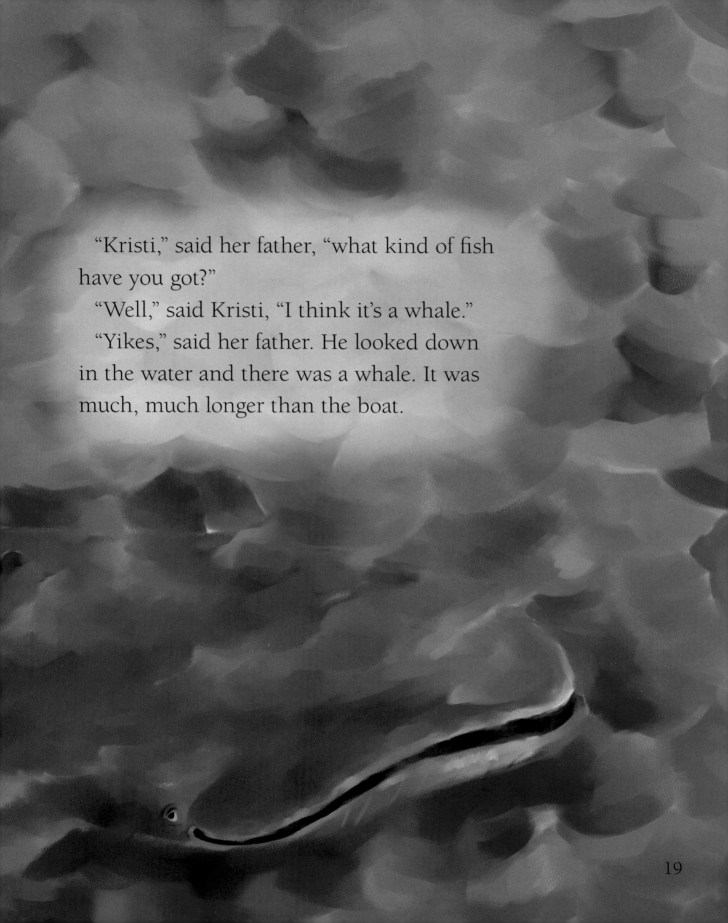

"Kristi," said her father, "what kind of fish have you got?"

"Well," said Kristi, "I think it's a whale."

"Yikes," said her father. He looked down in the water and there was a whale. It was much, much longer than the boat.

"Kristi," said her father, "let go of the whale."

"But it's a nice little whale," said Kristi. "I want to take it home and show it to Mommy."

"Kristi," said her father, "PLEEEASE let go of the whale."

So Kristi let go of the whale and her father took the boat back to Rocky Harbour.

Kristi's mother was waiting on the dock. Kristi said, "Look! Look! I fell in the ocean and caught this fish. Daddy threw me back in to catch another one, but it got away."

Her mother said, "Your father took you fishing?"

"Yes," said Kristi.

Her mother said, "You fell overboard?"

"Yes," said Kristi.

Her mother said, "Your father threw you back in the ocean?"

"Yes," said Kristi. "I love fishing!"

Kristi's mother looked at her father and said, "You threw her back in the ocean?"

"Yes," said her father.

Her mother yelled, "WHY?"

"Well," said her father, "she caught the biggest fish I have ever seen, so I threw her back in to get me another one."

"Right," said Kristi's mother. "If fish are so important, why don't you go get another one yourself."

And she picked up Kristi's father and threw him in the ocean.

Then Kristi and her mother had a big fish dinner and invited everyone in town.

And the next day, everybody went fishing.

To Kristi Parsons, Rocky Harbour, Newfoundland.
—R.M.

To my Dad, who has taught me many great things, like how
to fish . . . without throwing me in.
—M.B.

Scholastic Canada Ltd.
604 King Street West, Toronto, Ontario M5V 1E1, Canada

Scholastic Inc.
557 Broadway, New York, NY 10012, USA

Scholastic Australia Pty Limited
PO Box 579, Gosford, NSW 2250, Australia

Scholastic New Zealand Limited
Private Bag 94407, Botany, Manukau 2163, New Zealand

Scholastic Children's Books
Euston House, 24 Eversholt Street, London NW1 1DB, UK

www.scholastic.ca

Library and Archives Canada Cataloguing in Publication
Munsch, Robert N., 1945-, author
Get me another one! / by Robert Munsch ; illustrated by Mike Boldt.
ISBN 978-1-4431-6328-6 (softcover)
I. Boldt, Mike, illustrator II. Title.
PS8576.U575G48 2018   jC813'.54   C2017-904161-4

6 5 4 3 2 1   Printed in Malaysia 108   18 19 20 21 22